LESSONS I LEARNED FROM DRINKING

LESSONS

I LEARNED FROM DRINKING

Life Principles Gained Through Investing in Spirits

TIMOTHY L. FIELDS

Published in Nashville, Tennessee, by Heritage Publishing

Library of Congress Cataloging-in-Publishing
2017942270

ISBN 9780997431865

CONTENTS

DEDICATION

This book is dedicated to my two beautiful children, Miss Carter and Master Alexander, and to all of those people who have a dream or an idea or just want to share something with the world.

I have been working on this book for over ten years. I finally got tired of talking about it and started doing it, with the encouragement of friends and family. Whatever you desire to do, make it happen! The fact that you are reading this book means anything is possible if you put your mind to it.

FOREWORD

A former supervisor once told me, "Don't let college get in the way of your education." As the son of college administrators and a higher education professional myself, the truth of that statement is humorously intriguing to me. I find that the longer I live, the more that saying rings true.

Although I've spent almost 20 years in the classroom in some capacity, I've found that the most valuable knowledge I've gained has not, in fact, come from inside a classroom but rather from sitting at a bar (or around a campfire, at a cocktail party, or on a friend's back porch), drink in hand, talking with friends and processing life.

About ten years ago, I finished my course work for a PhD program and passed my comprehensive exams but had not completed a dissertation, which in academia is known as ABD (All But Dissertation). Since then, I've had plenty of time to complete it, but for any number of reasons, I have not done so. However, I have come up with a topic that I am passionate about.

I have conducted informal research (I can assure you, no human subjects were harmed in the writing of this book) and come to a couple of conclusions along the way that make up the foundation of this book. So while no one will call me Dr. Fields because I wrote this book, I hope this work provides at least some educational value.

What is this book *not* about? It's not actually about alcohol, nor does it celebrate alcoholism, which is a serious disease that affects many people. This book is a reflection on the valuable truths I have learned, the people who have been present in my life, and the decisions I've made (or avoided making), thanks in part to a drink in hand. This book contains a lot of storytelling mixed with stream-of-consciousness reflections that, hopefully, land on important guiding principles, which have helped me mature and evolve in a life that has no road map.

I know that without these valuable experiences, I would not be the person I am today. Some of the lessons learned were hard (and expensive). But they were necessary to make me someone I'm proud to be and to help me be at peace with myself. This book explores the challenges of living and learning from all the things life has thrown at me.

Hopefully, this book will make you laugh. More importantly, I hope you can relate to a story or two and then reflect on your own experiences. So pull up a chair, and order your drink of choice. Let's toast to life and all the lessons it teaches us!

INTRODUCTION

It was a Fuzzy Navel—peach Schnapps plus orange juice. That's the drink that did it. I was about 14 when my mother let me have a taste, and since then my life has never been the same. I can't tell you how many drinks I have consumed since that first sip; but I can tell you with great certainty that I have spent thousands and thousands of dollars on alcohol, because of alcohol, and as a result of what alcohol does.

While I would maybe like to rethink some of the decisions I've made and perhaps cut back on some of the money I've spent during those drinking escapades, I would not change a thing because some of the best and most meaningful life lessons I've learned have been as a result of those experiences. Truth be told, the outline of this book was written on a bar napkin after a long day at the Iron Horse Hotel in Milwaukee, Wisconsin, in the fall of 2008. (For what it's worth, if you're ever in Milwaukee, the Iron Horse is a great hotel, and there's an outstanding jazz bar right down the block.)

The purpose of this book is not to glorify or celebrate drinking. There are many people who don't drink or who have made the decision to stop drinking, and I applaud them for that choice. Instead, I wrote this book to share the importance of independence; self-awareness; good mental health; financial management; friendships; and, most notably, peace of mind. Hopefully, the lessons I've learned will help you as you deal with conflicts or find yourself standing at a crossroads.

The experiences you will read about in this book are not all from my personal life. This is a collection of personal and second-hand stories that serve as a record of some legendary and funny days and nights that I will never forget—and I have the bar tabs to prove it! So whether, like me, you are a lush who knows it is always happy hour somewhere and love the *Mad Men* lifestyle because they found nothing wrong with drinking Manhattans for breakfast, or you're someone who enjoys a good read while drinking those fancy coffees that cost as much as cocktails, I'm sure you'll find something within these pages that will make you laugh, think, and reflect.

At the end of each chapter, I have written a

reflection question and left room for notes. I hope you'll be an involved reader by asking yourself the questions, thinking through your answers, and using the spaces to jot down your responses and any additional thoughts you might have. Don't be surprised if you read a chapter at different times and you have different thoughts on the principles addressed. That's a reflection of the changes taking place in your life.

But before we begin, let's set the tone for our journey together. First, pour your favorite beverage. It doesn't matter if it's a Don Julio 1942 neat, as enjoyed by my favorite accountants who think there is no bad time to drink tequila, or a tall macchiato, which several of my colleagues drink daily because there is a Starbucks in the building. Then, make sure you pour yourself a glass of water. No matter what you drink, you always need more water.

Finally, put on some relaxing music. May I suggest Miles Davis's *Kind of Blue*? Then, sit back and let me tell you a few of the *Lessons I Learned From Drinking*—or at least the ones
I am willing to share.

WHAT'S YOUR FAVORITE NON-ALCOHOLIC BEVERAGE?

Chapter 1

YOU GET WHAT YOU PAY FOR

"When you're used to filet mignon,

. . . it's kinda hard to go back to

Hamburger Helper."—Jay Z ("Party Life")

Happy hour—3 PM to 7 PM, 6 PM to 10 PM, after work for the grown and sexy. They'll say anything to entice you for just one drink because usually that's all it takes. Happy hour—$2 martinis, $1 shots, or $20 buckets of beer. That's the ticket. Better yet, Fiesta Fridays with half-priced margaritas.

But have you read the fine print? It's the difference between a used car and a new one. It's the difference between Casamigos tequila and a well tequila, the Hamptons vs. the Jersey Shore, or Neiman Marcus vs. Walmart. It's the difference between a shirt hand-stitched from Turnbull & Asser on Jermyn Street in London, as opposed to one from Men's Wearhouse. (Nothing against Men's Wearhouse, but if I want to impress them in the boardroom, the detail on the Turnbull & Asser shirt could really seal the deal.)

As I was preparing to run down to Cancun for a brief session of rest, relaxation, and maybe some tequila, I purchased some inexpensive shirts from a retailer that shall remain nameless. What could be the harm? After spending time in the sun, playing golf, dining at exquisite restaurants, and drinking several shots, my short getaway ended. The life of the shirts seemed to be over as well. While the shirts packed well in the suitcase, unfortunately, they did not survive the initial rinse cycle via permanent press.

As I took the shirts from the washing machine, the observations were mystifying. After only one wash, a once-bright cyan shirt was four shades lighter than when I had purchased it, not to mention there was a long, loose thread that was unraveling as I removed the shirt from the washing machine. I saw two pieces of fabric separating like a couple who should have never been married in the first place.

Years ago, I purchased a used 2001 Honda Accord with 90,000 miles. At the time I bought it, it was ten years old. The mechanic said that the car was solid, so how could I go wrong with a Japanese car, especially if I wanted to purchase a used one? This was one of those things that made me say, "Hmmm?" I mean, I was saving 20 grand by opting not to purchase a brand-new car. For $5,000, what could go wrong?

Well, three months later, I found out. As I was entering the on-ramp to the highway at about 15 mph, my steering wheel locked. I could no longer control the direction the car was headed. As a result, the car continued to veer to the left and, ever so gently, the front of the driver's side of the car smashed into the guardrail. No one was harmed, but the cost to replace the steering column cost nearly as much as I paid for the car!

After a long week on the job, coworkers will get you every time with a simple "Let's grab a drink!" The bar near the job had happy hour every Thursday from 5 to 9 PM. They had a well-stocked bar of top-shelf liquors to choose from, but for the grown and sexy, they had $2 shot specials. You already know! I told the fellas at the job, "I got the first round."

So after much trash-talking with one another, with strangers who now called themselves "friends," and the bar staff who stood there and politely poured each round, the room began to spin. I can't recall what method of transportation was used to ensure my safe arrival home, but somehow I woke up the next day on my living room floor. (Notice, I did not indicate that it was morning when I woke up, although it was probably morning when I arrived there.)

Lesson learned: You get what you pay for. Maybe if I had opted to purchase shirts from Turnbull & Asser, the lovely cyan shirt would still be cyan and would still exist. Maybe if I had spent $20K, I wouldn't have been sitting off to the side of the on-ramp with a beautiful dent in my car. Likewise, if I had opted for top-shelf liquor instead of several—and I do mean several—$2 shots, I might not have experienced the pain in my head and the nausea. But enough about that. You get the picture. You get what you pay for in life.

We have so much more to discuss. Sip slowly . . .

WHAT'S SOMETHING THAT YOU WISH YOU HAD INVESTED IN MORE?

Chapter 2

LET IT OUT

"So tonight, gotta leave that nine-to-five upon the shelf and just enjoy yourself. Groove, let the madness in the music get to you. Life ain't so bad at all if you live it off the wall."
Michael Jackson ("Off the Wall")

As I approached my 40th birthday, there were a lot of things that I was proud of, but there were some moments that, perhaps, I wish I could have omitted. After a long night of drinking, more times than I care to admit, I have felt the need to relieve myself in some form in order to get to sleep—or as a friend of mine says, "Fight off a bad case of the whirlies [the birds that fly around your head when you're dizzy]."

The older I get, the more I realize that I have to listen to my body. I've found out the hard way that sometimes your body will naturally and instinctively relieve itself. Other times, this process has to be induced. Either way, there comes a point when you have to do what you have to do. I've had to get "it" out, one way or another so I could feel better and sleep for the next day. I'm not saying this because it's a source of pride or because I ever want to experience this. But the reality is, it happens. And once you are there, you have to figure out what you are going to do.

The most recent incident, or shall I say the time I am willing to share, happened while I was catching up with friends in Washington, DC. What started out as meeting up for casual drinks off U Street ended up looking like an excerpt from *The Hangover* movies, Parts I, II, and III. On most nights like this, there is usually that moment when the little person on my shoulder says, "Enough is enough!" or asks, "What the hell are you doing?" And on this night, that happened around 2:00 AM. At that same moment, I realized that I had not eaten anything for 12 hours. Epic fail!

When I was younger, I used to think you could only get drunk by consuming too much alcohol. Actually, there are numerous ways you can get drunk that have less to do with the amount you drink and more to do with factors such as what you've eaten, how much water you've had, whether you're drinking cheap liquor, or if you mix light and dark liquors. Any number of things can expedite the intoxication process beyond simply the amount of alcohol consumed. It's also important to remember that moderation has its place.

Needless to say, at 2:00 AM, it was beyond time for me to go. But rather than going to find something to eat (and trust me, there is nothing healthy to eat at that time of morning),

I just caught a Lyft to my hotel to get some rest. Once I arrived at my hotel room, I convinced myself that if I took a shower and drank some water, it would be all good. But before I could try to sober up, my body decided it was time to "let it out." I knew that needed to happen, but I was in denial about the possibility of it happening as I was preparing to lie down with a trash can next to the bed.

Once my body relieved itself, I felt a little better and was happy to get some of those toxins out so I could fall asleep. Of course, the next morning was a little rough, but not as rough as the night before.

Like drinking, life presents us with any number of issues that can inhibit our ability to function at our full potential in our work environments, relationships, and family responsibilities. When we are faced with these occurrences, how do we deal with them? Do we talk about them and find healthy outlets? Or do we internalize them, pretend they're no big deal, ignore them, or lash out?

More often than not, we do nothing; and after so much time, these small day-to-day things can add up. Before you know it, stress, anger, fatigue, resentment, or other emotions have set in.

There comes a time when we have to let these feeling and energy out in some way. There are many ways people can let it out. Some of my favorite methods include exercise, writing or journaling, therapy, and masturbation. Whatever way you choose, you have to find a healthy way to let it out, because if you continue to hold these things in, they will become toxic and cancerous. Sooner or later, your body will let you know that enough is enough, and it won't be as simple to clean up as taking a shower, eating a meal, taking medicine, drinking water, or whatever most people do to alleviate their hangovers.

Just like the hangover that comes after a long night of drinking, you might have collateral damage after letting it out. You might need to mend relationships, have difficult conversations that are long overdue, reevaluate life goals, and maybe end a friendship or a partnership. Ultimately, you have to take care of you, because if you don't take care of you, you can't help anyone else.

A couple of years ago, a friend stopped by my office to say hello, but her visit quickly turned into a venting session about her mom, her new husband, and several other things that had her feeling lost and resentful. I listened to her for about 30 minutes and then had to stop her and ask a few questions.

"When was the last time you were on an airplane?"

Puzzled, she said, "About a month ago. Why?"

I mentioned the presentation that the flight attendants give before takeoff. "What do you do when the mask drops and you have your son with you?"

"I put mine on first," she said. Then she smiled and said, "I get it, Tim! I have to take care of me first."

I was happy she had taken the time to express herself, but she was venting to the wrong person. She needed to be expressing these frustrations to her husband and her mother so they could understand her feelings of exasperation.

Letting it out is just a necessity of life. While I'm making light of the process of relieving myself after a long night of drinking, the reality is that we all know of times when we have had to just get something off our chests and then felt a lot better after we did it. Whether we're venting to friends about something they did to upset us, arguing with a partner about not making up the bed, or letting out a yell before a workout, it is imperative to just let it out.

I would argue that keeping things bottled up is worse than the many unhealthy toxins you ingest after drinking because many times bottled-up feelings cause stress, resentment, anger, hurt, and other ill effects. These are not beneficial and can affect your physical and mental health as well as your peace of mind. Life is too short to keep things bottled up, so find a way to express yourself, and let it out so you can rest well without the whirly birds, nausea, fatigue, and bullshit that life can sometimes bring.

WHEN WAS THE LAST TIME YOU FELT THE NEED TO RELEASE SOMETHING?

Chapter 3

KNOW YOUR ENEMY

"Alcohol may be man's worst enemy, but the Bible says love your enemy." Frank Sinatra

Gin is not my friend.

If you go out to enough social gatherings where alcohol is involved, you will have plenty of opportunities to taste any number of spirits. But, as in life, drinking it all can become a matter of trial and error to find out what works best for you. In my trial and error, I found that gin does not work for me.

I have a lot of friends (many of whom are from England or who spend a great deal of time in Europe or who grew up listening to too much Snoop Dogg) who have told me about the complex and pronounced flavors that exist in the taste of a good gin, and they try to convince me that I should give it one more try. But it doesn't matter. Gin and I don't agree. I had to learn that the hard way.

As a young professional in my early 20s, I went through a phase where if it was wet and the right price, I would drink it. As I developed a more "sophisticated" palate (in other words, I started to make more money), I was heavily influenced by clever marketing campaigns to drink the finer spirits, so I have had more than my fair share of Cîroc. As time went on, I was not as worried about name or cost but rather about how it was made; how it tasted; and, most importantly, if it agreed with me.

Gin is not on that list!

So what did gin do to me? Beat me down to the ground?

In my early 20s, the broke days, I was out with friends at your average house party. There was good music, cards, dominos, and a lot of women. While many of the parties I attend now have a healthy selection of spirits, chasers, and food, this party had music; chicken wings; a big bottle of cheap gin; and your choice of chaser, orange juice or cranberry juice, neither of which contained any real juice. Despite this, I thought that party had it all and was excited about all of the possibilities.

I knew as soon as I saw the bottle that I was not a fan of gin, but given the setting, I figured, *Why not? What's the worst that could happen?* I thought that if I put enough juice in it, I wouldn't even taste it. As the night went on, everything seemed fine until things began to go south. Without going into a lot of detail, let's just say that the night didn't end well, and I was sick for two days. I didn't want to eat or drink anything. No one could say it wasn't the gin; but I couldn't say it was the chicken, the cheap juice, or the amount of gin I had consumed.

No, it was the gin.

Fast forward almost 20 years, and I was told that if I drank a certain "fine" cocktail with gin, such as a French 75, I wouldn't even taste it and my feelings about gin would change. Given the amount of time that passed, I kept an open mind and tried it. At the first sip, I started to feel sick and went back to that dark place I had experienced 20 years earlier. I didn't drink anything else that night, so you know it was serious! Gin and I just don't agree, and I'm fine with that.

I may not get along with gin, but I have some friends who run from tequila and other spirits as fast as they can and, believe it or not, I have friends who just don't drink. (They prefer to partake in other things, but that's another book in the making.) Whatever the case, it is important to know with what and with whom you don't agree and to stay clear of them.

On a beautiful Sunday afternoon, I stopped by one of my favorite margarita places for what I thought would be a quick drink and some down time spent enjoying the day. A friend of mine, who happened to be in the neighborhood, stopped by for a drink, too. She ordered the same thing I was drinking, and we toasted to Sunday Funday and life. We made sure to look each other in the eyes as we toasted because there's a belief that if you do not maintain eye contact throughout the toast, you will be relegated to seven years of bad sex. I don't think it's true, but I don't want to take that chance.

After two hours of entertaining conversation and two, three, maybe four margaritas, we decided we needed food. We went to a Tex/Mex eatery next door and ate dinner, and the margaritas kept flowing. What we thought was just going to be a drink and some friendly conversation turned into a five-hour drinking marathon. Finally, the night ended, and we said our goodbyes.

The next day, my friend texted me and said, "You can keep that nasty worm juice," along with all kinds of angry emojis. "Never again, Timmy!"

I texted her back and reminded her that she was the one who had ordered all those drinks, not me. I may have ordered a couple, but we were both in the moment. My only consolation to her was that at least we were drinking good tequila. Apparently, though, she and tequila have a checkered history and aren't friends. So I'm not sure what possessed her to drink so many margaritas that day.

But when she said, "Never again," she meant it. Since then, we've met up several times for drinks, but she makes sure there are other options beyond tequila. She even went so far as to tell me that I'm not her friend if I ever let her drink tequila again. My rebuttal to that was, "Grown folks do what they want to do."

One of my closest friends is successful in many areas, and some would argue that he has it all. But he messed around and fell in love with the wrong woman, so those who saw the perfect picture from the outside looking in did not see the constant dysfunction that was going on behind closed doors. We've all been there. Some people just don't need to be together on any level, no matter how much they think they enjoy each other's company.

It is always difficult to advise friends about matters of the heart, but several of us tried to tell him in different ways, but he was too far gone. And the worst part about it was that he knew she was not good for him, but he kept going back for more.

This relationship went on for years and had several ups and downs, some even involved legal separation. One day, we were out for drinks, and he said, "Tim, I need to leave her alone. She is my kryptonite." At first, I laughed at the kryptonite reference, but he was serious and finally acknowledged that the woman was not good for him. He did not leave her anytime soon. But a few years later, he finally did leave and is now in a much better place. I would say that now he does have everything!

Enemies come in all forms, but if you do not know which yours are, how will you stay clear of them to avoid the negative outcomes that they will present you? Is it gambling, drinking, drugs, social media, food, or a former partner that you just can't say no to? I have been guilty of all of the above. Life is hard enough to navigate without directly engaging with people or things that can be detrimental. Identification of your enemies is imperative in order to live a peaceful and successful life, so the more you know about these areas, the better you can be prepared to stay clear of them.

Gin is not my friend, nor will it ever be. I had to find that out the hard way. That woman was my friend's kryptonite for years, and he went through a lot before he came to that realization. There are any number of ways to describe an enemy, but only you know yours.

Who or what is your enemy? Find it, identify it, and stay clear of it at all cost!

Gin is not my friend.

Water is my friend.

Lyft is my friend.

We will talk about friends more down the road, but let us continue our journey. How's that cup looking?

WHO OR WHAT IS YOUR ENEMY?

Chapter 4

IT'S OK TO WALK AWAY

"Don't look so sad. I know it's over. But life goes on, and this world keeps on turning. Let's just be glad we have this time to spend together." Al Green ("For the Good Times")

"I bet you won't . . ." "I dare you to . . ." These words are uttered by people issuing a challenge. Many times, the challenge is something quite harmless and innocent, but there are other times when that is not the case.

And when it comes to drinking, these words are uttered all too often. "I bet you won't take a shot." "I bet you won't take one more drink." "I bet you won't ________." Just fill in the blank. You know you've been there, and so have I. On so many nights, I gave in to peer pressure to have one more drink or to take a shot when I knew I didn't want either one. Rather than just say no, I took the challenge and suffered the consequences (let it out).

So what's so hard about saying no and just walking away from the situation? Why do we feel the need to prove ourselves, especially when we are around friends and family and our actions would not change their view of us? Is it ego? pride? a need to be accepted? fear?

I am not a fan of shots, as I will remind you throughout this book, along with the fact that I don't like gin. But I have probably taken more of them in my lifetime than I should have, and each and every one of them hurt going down, always followed by an ugly face. So why do I do it? Because part of me doesn't want to look like I can't handle it or be called a punk. But a larger part of me just wants to enjoy the moment with those who enjoy shots. It's hard to say no when a round of 20 shots comes to the table and your whole crew lifts the glasses to celebrate life. Who wants to be on the sideline for that?

But as I've gotten older and wiser, I've learned to say no and stop caring about how I may be perceived or about what is said when I refuse to partake. Most of the time, whatever is said is lighthearted and fun.

But when alcohol is involved, there is always the potential for things to get heated and for people to say things they would not have said otherwise. Just take the good with the bad, and walk away.

On a side note, I believe that "a drunken tongue is a truthful one." Usually, what people say under the influence is true, whether they want to admit it or not. I have learned to walk away from these shot sessions when one after the other comes to the table. I have also learned to keep my mouth shut when I have been drinking. If that's your thing, go for it. As I've gotten older, maybe I don't feel the need to prove myself as I did when I was younger, or maybe I'm just tired of the burn as the shots go down. Either way, I have become comfortable enough in my own skin to say, "I'm good."

Much of my ability to walk away from these shot sessions has less to do with what's going on and more about me learning to be comfortable in my own skin, putting what's in my best interest ahead of the pressure to drink or prove myself, and not being overly concerned with what other people think or say. If I take those shots, I alone am responsible for whatever happens, thus I should make the decision about what I will or will not do instead of being swayed by others.

This concept of learning the ability to say no holds

true in life as well. In the past few years, I have been in many conversations about divorce and separation. While divorce, unfortunately, seems to be the new norm, with almost 50 percent of marriages ending in divorces, talking about it isn't easy. Many of these conversations center on money, kids, fear, and several other factors that influence marriage beyond love that are often complicated and require a lot of soul searching.

But, often, what's missing from the conversation is what is best for the individual. People are so concerned about perceptions, ego, pride, and fear that they rarely talk about what is best for them as an individual. And just like when the round of shots comes, many times we take that shot as opposed to walking away and not worrying about what others may say or how they may perceive us.

Walking away from any relationship, job, financial failure, or friendship is hard, but doing so is not an admission of failure. Rather, it's simply an acknowledgment that the situation is no longer what's best for you. I'm not suggesting that anytime something gets hard that you just say "Forget it" and walk away. I'm simply saying that there should be a lot of thought given to what's best for you, the individual, in that moment and not so much about what's best for the situation in the long-term.

About five years ago, I was faced with the decision of whether to foreclose on my first house or to continue to pay money into it while its value plummeted. I went back and forth for months, worried about my credit, where I would live, and what it would say about me if I walked away.

Finally, after about six months of going back and forth, I decided that I couldn't do it anymore, knowing the value would never come back, and I let the house go. I walked through it one last time, thinking of all the great memories, but I didn't look back. I was no longer worried about what would happen next.

Six months later, I came to my new residence and found a UPS envelope under my doormat. I thought it was a bill, so I just put it to the side. A few days later, I finally opened it. The envelope held a check for a little over $10,000. Apparently, all those months I was going back and forth, they had already started the foreclosure process and returned the money I was paying for that time.

I invested the money in something that is much more valuable than that house, or anything on this earth, and that will never depreciate in value. This wouldn't have happened if I had stayed in the house and concerned myself with the "what if's." When one door closes, another door opens, but you have to be willing to make that walk if it's right for you.

Am I done taking shots? No, I'm sure I will have one sooner rather than later. But I'm happy to know that I will be making the decision and not be influenced by anything or anyone, and that feels good. It's OK to walk away, but once you do, make sure you look forward and be prepared for all the good things that are ahead.

FROM WHAT OR FROM WHOM HAVE YOU HAD TO WALK AWAY?

Chapter 5

KNOW YOUR FRIENDS

"Friends, how many of us have them?" Whodini ("Friends")

By now, you know that I'm not a fan of shots, but I still take them from time to time. Why? Sometimes I get caught up in the moment, as many of us do. But most times, I take shots when I'm with one of my closest friends, who loves shots and is the primary inspiration for the previous chapter. I would hate to see how much we collectively have spent on liquor over the course of our 20-plus years of friendship. It might be enough to fund a small country.

My friend enjoys shots, and whenever he gets the opportunity, he encourages me and anyone around to enjoy a shot or two with him. (I have seen people drink way too much trying to keep pace with him, including my sister-in-law, who went toe-to-toe with him once and lived to tell the story. She was very proud.)

But while these shot sessions are taking place, my friend usually makes sure I get only half of what everyone else is getting, or he will divert attention from the fact that I have not taken my shot and will put pressure on someone else to take it. That person is the one who usually falls for the "I bet you won't . . ." challenge.

In those moments, I value how my friend makes sure he is enjoying himself but also ensures that I don't feel any unnecessary pressure to participate, and he doesn't make an issue of it if I say no. There are many reasons he and I have had a great friendship over the past 20-some years, but this is one of the little things that separates the real from the fake in my eyes and has kept us close.

In this technologically driven society, where everyone is a friend and people can express themselves on any number of social networks, it's hard to find out who is in your corner. People can like everything you do on social media and actually not know anything about you.

Sometimes, I find myself in these awkward spaces when people approach me, and it is clear that they know me and we have a relationship on some level, but I simply can't place their names in that moment. It's nothing personal. I just know a lot of people, and I'm not good with names, especially when drinking is involved.

I have such a hard time remembering names that my wife, bless her heart, came up with a way to help me out, because heaven knows I need it in so many ways. So now when people approach me and its obvious I don't know their names, I will say, "This is my wife," and she will then say, "I did not catch your name." (Don't tell anyone our secret.) As to my inability to remember names, my wife just shakes her head and says, "You're welcome—again!" The reality is, there are only about 50 people I call friends. The rest are associates or colleagues, or they fall into a general category of "people I know."

Hopefully, what I'm saying is not coming across as arrogant. I'm only providing context to how I see the word *friend*, a word that is seriously overused in our society.

Often, when I post a picture of friends on social media, it's followed by #nonewfriends to highlight how important these lifelong friendships are and the loyalty that serves as the foundation of many of these relationships. Some friends tease me by saying that I do make new friends. They're right, and I'm still open to that. But my hashtag means that I usually gravitate to those friends I grew up with because they know me best, and I don't need help remembering their names.

One of my favorite places to visit is New Orleans. I try to get there at least twice a year or more if I can. I think it is one of the few places in the United States that has its own culture that transcends race, socioeconomics, and the many factors that limit our ability to connect on a human level with those who may be different.

Every time I go to New Orleans, I find something new and fall more in love with the people, culture, and food (jambalaya, shrimp stew, po' boys, and crawfish étouffée, just to name a few local favorites). While this is my experience, most people identify New Orleans with Bourbon Street and Mardi Gras, which I had the pleasure of attending not too long ago. However, there is so much more to that charming city than a single event and street.

It's hard to describe in words, but if you've been to New Orleans, you know what I'm talking about. If you have not been there, you should step away from reading and book a trip as soon as possible. And when you get there, visit Tales of the Cocktail. That is a must-do for anyone who enjoys a great cocktail or the "art of drinking."

About ten years ago, I was on Bourbon Street at 3:00 AM, making my way back to my hotel, and I saw a guy propped up against a wall. If you know anything about Bourbon Street, you know that sitting on or even touching the ground is not something you want to do—ever—especially late at night. This guy was inebriated but was now asleep and sitting in his own vomit. (I guess he had to let it out.) I couldn't help wondering, *Where are his friends? How could real friends just leave him out here like this?*

I don't know exactly why that guy was still out there, but I know that my true friends would never have let that happen to me. I have had a lot of rough nights, but when I am with my true friends, I never have to worry. No matter what happens, we are going to take care of one another and make sure everyone is safe. "No man or woman left behind." That's the code.

Not long ago, I was talking to a friend who was going through a transitional time in her life as it related to some of her closest childhood friends and family. She was feeling as if she could not be the person she was becoming as a young adult and that those closest to her would only accept her for the person she was as a teenager and a college student. While it was vital that she maintained these relationships, she also wanted to feel accepted, as we all do. She was at a crossroads as to how to be comfortable in her new identity but still maintain those relationships that had been so important to her for so long.

I knew I did not have the answers to her situation. She was going to have to figure out what was best for her, as well as how to manage those relationships moving forward.

I try my best to stay clear of offering advice on matters of the heart because it's usually a no-win proposition. But what I could tell her was that all of the people I call friends and most of my family have fallen out at some point in time—sometimes for a few days and, in other instances, for years. That's just part of being in long-term relationships. But although we've fallen out from time to time, we are still close, if not closer, to this day. In many cases, we are better friends due to experiencing these differences.

The people who care about you and love you are going to do so no matter what. Those who are not in your corner will get stuck in their feelings or find some shallow reason to write you off. But that's OK because it gives you a chance to see who's really in your corner. Friendship is a two-way street. It's good to know who your friends are, but it's just as important to be a good friend in return. If we're all honest, we could probably improve in the area of friendships.

I never understood the concept of being a wingman, but one night while out with a friend, I found out what was required of the job on the fly. The two of us were hanging out at a hidden speakeasy in Atlanta and were enjoying some overpriced "craft" cocktails in a smoke-filled cigar bar. After a few rounds, we—meaning he—struck up a conversation with a couple of women. What began as a light conversation escalated quickly between my friend and one of the women.

After a couple more rounds, I noticed that my friend was getting a little too comfortable for his relationship status, so I decided to intervene and let him know that it was time for us to close out our tab and head to the house. I was met with some resistance ("Why you hating?"), but it's what needed to happen.

As we were on our way home, he thanked me for getting him out of that situation because, admittedly, he knew he had lost control. While we sometimes wonder what could have happened that night, we know the evening ended as it should have—at home, where we needed to be with the people we needed to be with.

So who are your friends? Who are the people who are going to take care of you, no matter what? Who is going to tell you the truth when you don't want to hear it? Who is going to just listen when you need to vent? Who is going to let you know when you are wrong? Who is going to make sure you are taken care of at the end of the day?

These are important questions, and only you can answer them because you don't want to be that guy propped up on Bourbon Street. Neither do you want to be that person who is surrounded by people who don't have your best interests at heart. Knowing your friends is more than just knowing who is in your corner. It's about knowing who is going to help build you, challenge you, and help you grow. With each year comes different challenges, but it's critical to know who is there for you and not for their own personal benefit, or who will bail or turn their backs when things get rough.

Just as you need to know your enemies, it's just as important to know who your true friends are. It's often said, "Keep your friends close and your enemies closer." Just because you enjoy someone's company doesn't mean that person is your friend. Make it a point to be able to know the difference between people you know and people who are going to make sure you are safe, comfortable, and aware of what's going on.

So who are your friends? Who is on your team? Who is in your corner? If you don't know, you better find out because that round of 20 shots is coming, as well as trying times when you need people who are there to ensure you are OK.

WHO HAS YOUR BACK NO MATTER WHAT?

Chapter 6

BE CONSISTENT

"Champagne with breakfast while I'm yawning. You can't drink all day if you don't start in the morning." Drake ("Signs")

I have heard that consistency is the key to life. But while consistency is important, it doesn't always guarantee success. Instead, when you are consistent, you're usually in a much better place to be successful in your endeavors.

All of my life, I have been a runner. The more consistent I am at running, the better my life is overall. Currently, I am a middle-aged road warrior who tries to run between 10-20 miles a week. But in my prime as a student at Morehouse College in Atlanta, Georgia, I was an accomplished All-American runner in cross country and track and field. While I enjoyed both sports, cross country was my true passion. I love smelling the morning dew, being in the natural elements, and seeing all the topography that makes up a cross-country course.

During most of my career at Morehouse, I was one of the top long-distance runners in the region. I was by no means the fastest or the most gifted runner, but I always prided myself on putting in the work necessary to be successful. I was an unrecruited walk-on who had to earn a scholarship, but I was successful because I made it a priority to be consistent in my daily work ethic.

Most college cross-country courses are five miles or 10K (6.2 miles), and any good coach will tell you that the key to winning is consistency in your mile pace. I can't tell you how many times that adrenaline has gotten the best of runners as they passed that first mile-marker well under the pace they trained for, just to have their next mile blow up and be well above the pace they were trying to maintain. And with over three miles to go, it usually doesn't get any better. Most runners would prefer not to be the first person through the first mile-marker for that reason.

It was always my goal to try to hit each mile right around five-minute splits. I knew if I did that,

I would be in the mix at the end of the race. I cannot say that I won or event-placed in every race, but toward the end of my time at Morehouse, I won much more than I lost. And learning consistency was a vital component to that success.

Like running, I also learned the importance of consistency after many rough nights of drinking whatever was placed in front of me. One night, I started drinking wine, switched to vodka, and ended the night with a Scotch or champagne. My body was like, "What the hell are you doing, and why?" In those moments, I was like, "It's what's being served," "It's free," or any number of legitimate but stupid reasons to drink what's in front of me.

As my palate has evolved, I have learned that if I start with a drink, I should stick with that drink through the day or night. I would recommend that you stay with the same drink for the duration; but if you must switch, keep it in the same family. For example, if you are drinking white spirits such as vodka, white rum, or gin, stay there and don't switch to bourbon midstream, because that's when things usually go bad—whether you want to admit it or not. I have found that if I keep my cocktails or drinks consistent, I have enjoyed my nights out much more and, like my running career, I am in the mix at the end more times than not.

As you have probably gathered by this point in the book, I have had a lot of long nights of drinking, and I also like to enjoy myself whenever the opportunity presents itself. Part of the reason for writing this book is to reflect on the many good times I have had, but I also want to share what I have learned through my bad experiences, too. As I think back on those many nights, I can say that there are several memorable ones, especially the night that came to be known as The Night of the Triple Dog Dare.

The Night of the Triple Dog Dare took place in the late 1990s in Buckhead, an affluent neighborhood in Atlanta. I went out with one of my female cousins visiting from LA and one of my closest friends from college for what I thought was going to be a casual night of drinking and catching up. But this was not going to be the case.

Now to really appreciate this story, you have to know that these two people, whom I love dearly, are highly competitive, very opinionated, rarely wrong about anything, and stubborn as hell (and both of them have a mean streak). When the waitress first greeted us and asked what we were drinking, before my cousin could say a word, my friend promptly responded, "I will have whatever she's having!"

My cousin said, "You really want to do that?" to which my friend replied, "I ain't scared."

At that point, I said, "I will take some water," and took a front-row seat to the next four hours of foolishness.

They enjoyed the first round, and then my cousin called the waitress over.

"We will take another round, as well as a dozen oysters as well, please."

Apparently, she knew that there is something that oysters do when mixed with alcohol that can potentially speed up the process of intoxication. Since she was drinking her drink of choice, she believed that she already had an advantage, but my friend had no clue. After 48 oysters, five rounds between them, and a lot of shit-talking, we got the bill. Neither of them were in good shape, but neither was willing to back down or wave the white flag.

Being the responsible one that night, I decided it was time to put both of them out of their misery. The plan was to drop off my friend at his house downtown and then head to Marietta, a suburb north of Atlanta, where my cousin and I were staying at her mother's house for the night.

As we were making our way downtown, my friend said that he had to use the bathroom, so I found a vacant parking lot, and he found a secluded place to relieve himself. But in a fit of unsolicited rage that must have been building up through the night with all the back-and-forth banter, my cousin ran after him, cussing him out. All I can say is that my friend was running and peeing while my cousin chased him and cussed him out, which was hilarious, except for the fact that I had to break up the fight.

Once we made it back to the car, I dropped off my friend before making the 30-minute drive from downtown Atlanta to Marietta with my cousin. You can probably guess who slept the entire ride. Once we made it to the house at around 3:00 AM, my cousin said she had to use the bathroom. After 30 minutes, I went to check on her, and she assured me she was OK, so I went to sleep. The next morning when I woke up, her mother's first question to me was, "Why was my 30-year-old daughter asleep next to the toilet all night?" As you can imagine, I did not have a good answer.

As I reflect on that night years later, two things stand out. First, my friend was arrogant (he still is) and showed no restraint or consistency in what worked for him by letting my cousin determine his pace and, ultimately, the outcome of his evening. Second, alcohol mixed with pride makes even the smartest people do stupid things.

Consistency is more than the act of being diligent and steadfast. Instead, it speaks to brand management. How do you present yourself to the world? In many instances, your actions determine how people will see you. In a world that is overrun with brands trying to separate themselves from one another, you have to ask yourself, *Which ones are the most successful, and why are they successful?* The ones that are constantly trying to reinvent themselves based on the latest trends, or the ones that are committed to their values and principles and refuse to be influenced by others?

In the mid-1980s, at the height of their global success, Coca-Cola, one of the world's top companies, introduced a product called New Coke. As part of a rebranding process, the company introduced New Coke, which consisted of a formula different from the one that was responsible for much of the success of the company.

The product was a major failure that was vehemently rejected by the public. After months of trying to push this new product, Coca-Cola decided it was not working and went back to the original formula, which they dubbed Coca-Cola Classic. This move helped the company to rebound from a major setback. Coca-Cola is big enough and has enough capital to come back from a setback, but can you make such a mistake with your image or branding?

Be consistent. If you think back to times when you fell short of your goals, whether it was a job, a diet, a workout plan, a relationship, or remaining sober, were you consistent? Did you stay true to what you knew was best for you? Only you know what's best for you and what you are able to do, and it's critical that you stay true to that. Remember, your reputation follows you forever.

If you need to hit that five-minute mile, make sure you hit it, not 4:50 and not 5:15. If you need to drink your drink and you know the formula that works for you, then make sure you follow that path and do not stray. Your consistency will keep you at the top of your game and in the best position to be successful in all facets of life or just enough to make it through the night.

My glass is empty, so let me get a refill. You good?

IN WHAT AREA OF YOUR LIFE DO YOU THINK YOU NEED TO BE MORE CONSISTENT?

Chapter 7

TAKE A BREAK

"Run away as fast as you can." Kanye West ("Runaway")

Sometimes, we need to take a break and step out of the matrix. Often, we get caught up in work, relationships, rearing children, habits, and life in general, and we fail to take a break. Taking a break does not necessarily mean you have to take a vacation or run away (even though I am writing this portion of the book on a flight to Nassau to do both). Sometimes taking a break can mean stepping out of a three-hour meeting for five minutes just to collect your thoughts or taking a long drive after a heated conversation with a partner or a friend because you don't want to say or do something you will regret later.

There are many ways to take breaks, depending on the situation, but we all need them, no matter how we choose to take them. By taking a break, you are not just stepping away for a second, but you are giving yourself time to reflect, gather your thoughts, reassess what's going on, and prepare mentally for what's next. But there are also times when just taking a break will not help, and you have to hit control–alt–delete and walk away.

If you drink long enough, you will have days when you need to take a break as well. If you don't, your body will force you to take one, so it's best to build breaks in if you know you will be drinking for a long time. These events can start out as tailgating parties, bachelor or bachelorette parties, family reunions, grilling at the house with friends, or a quick drink after a long day that ended up being five hours of drinking and talking before you knew what happened.

Yes, I've had some long drinking days, as you can imagine. Some of them were intentional, but others just happened. In all instances, intentional or not, comes a point where it's best to step away, drink some water, take a walk, get some fresh air, or just stop. Too often when drinking, we drink, drink, drink; go, go, go;

and, yes, shot, shot, shot. But we fail to pay attention to the signs our bodies are giving us that we need to slow down or stop. We're so caught up in the moment or worried about what others will think of us that we can't even think about slowing down or walking away.

Every year, I know I will have at least one day when I will be drinking for the better part of the day—homecoming at my alma mater. At some homecomings, the drinking started as early as 7 AM and went throughout the day and into the night. These early mornings are usually on the heel of a long night that maybe ended at 3 or 4 AM. In my younger days, I used to go until I could not go any more. But as I've grown older and wiser and learned some hard lessons, I have learned to take periodic breaks throughout the day.

These breaks have allowed me not only to better enjoy the day, but they have also limited the stupid things I did and said while I was drinking. Some of these breaks consisted of making sure I drank water throughout the day and walked around so that I didn't remain stationary for long periods of time. But sometimes I just sat my ass down. Through the years, these breaks have become a welcome part of the day and have enhanced my overall experience and how I felt the next day.

As in life, just like drinking, we sometimes can get so caught up in the moment that we forget to enjoy the moment. At his NFL Hall of Fame induction speech, the great Jerry Rice talked about how he never took a break to enjoy all of the accomplishments he had achieved:

> If I have a single regret about my career standing here today, it's that I never took the time to enjoy it. I swear to God this is true because I was always working. Right after the season, whether we won the Super Bowl or not, I would take two weeks off and go right back to training.

Rice is right. There are great things that happen in our lives each day that we may miss out on because we don't take a moment to step away. This could be something as small as a conversation with a friend or as big as the birth of a child.

It's important that we prioritize so we don't let life pass us by.

At the end of the day, all we have is today, and it's incumbent upon us not to get so caught up in the destination that we don't enjoy the ride and the view along the way, smell the roses, or do any of the other hundreds of clichés that support this sentiment.

Since we are talking about breaks, let me get some water. Excuse me.

WHEN DID YOU LAST TAKE A BREAK?

Chapter 8

TAKE YOUR TIME

"Turn 'em off." Teddy Pendergrass ("Turn Off the Lights")

One night, I was with one of my closest friends at Taqueria del Sol, one of my favorite Mexican restaurants and watering holes in Atlanta. My friends and I were enjoying conversation over a pitcher, or two, of margaritas when one of the owners walked by. He is originally from Colombia, so he knows a thing or two about tequila. We stopped him and asked him about the more than 50 tequilas they offered.

"Which one do you think is best?"

"To sip or to shoot?" he asked. "If you are going to shoot it, pick the cheapest shit up there because the taste doesn't matter. But most of the tequilas we have were meant to sip and enjoy."

While that was more information than we anticipated, it did drive home a significant point. Most of the finer spirits are meant to be enjoyed and not just thrown back, so why not take your time and enjoy? What's the rush?

That conversation with the owner made me think about the many connoisseurs of spirits, wines, and beers whose sole purpose is to educate consumers on how these drinks are made and the best way to enjoy them. If you've ever been to a tasting for beer, wines, and spirits, you know that the aficionados can spend hours highlighting the multiple flavors, colors, tones, textures, and smells as they encourage you to take your time to enjoy the experience of the drink.

But those of us who have attended tastings are in the minority when it comes to alcohol consumers based upon numbers. Few of us care all that much about the process or how it is made. We just want to drink, overlooking the care and attention that goes into how many wines, beers, ciders, and spirits are made. But how can you enjoy them if you are just throwing them back?

Years ago, I attended a Johnnie Walker tasting to learn more about their Scotch whiskey.

Unfortunately, the men next to me were just there to taste the Blue Label. When it finally came out, they shot it like it was cheap tequila and walked out. Following their immediate exit, the aficionado spent the next 30 minutes explaining the many complex flavors of the Blue Label product, as well as the aging process, which clearly those men who left couldn't have cared less about.

Have I told you I am not a fan of shots? My conversation with the restaurant owner about the tequilas gave me another reason not to like them. Because of what he told us, it occurred to me that sometimes we need to take our time and enjoy a good drink and all that went into it, from the beginning of the process to the point where it's poured into the glass.

When I was younger, I was in such a hurry. I accumulated all kinds of speeding tickets and was involved in car accidents because I wasn't paying attention. My car insurance was extraordinarily high, almost to the point that it cost as much as my car note, which is ridiculous. When I think back to my younger days, I have come to the realization that the places I was in a hurry to go were not going anywhere. And in many instances, it wasn't work or places where I needed to be in the first place. I've come to realize that there is no need to be in such a hurry.

As a father who spends a lot of time in Atlanta traffic (there is always traffic) driving my kids to school, I see road rage, accidents, and people getting tickets for driving alone in the HOV lane. When I see these instances, I laugh and think about one of my favorite lines from the movie *Shawshank Redemption*. When the character Brooks was released from jail after 50 years, he said, "The world went and got itself in a big damn hurry."

Brooks was talking about how much the country changed in the span of 50 years while he was locked away. But it makes me want to ask those people who are always in a hurry, "Is wherever you're going worth getting a ticket and insurance increases, putting yourself and others on the road at risk, or potentially damaging your car?" I don't think it is, and nowadays I'm like Lionel Richie, "easy like Sunday morning," as I ride in the far-right lane.

As I think about the "joy" of driving, I reflect on my younger days, long before cellphones and our newfound addiction to social media. One of my favorite things to do was to go on Sunday rides. My father would load us up in the car and drive without a destination while we enjoyed the scenery, had conversations, laughed, and listened to some good music. Perhaps a long Sunday ride isn't your thing, but you can still find ways to disconnect from the matrix.

I've had friends tell me about how they are over-scheduled and how sick they are of their phones, which is constantly going off with text messages and e-mails. My response? "You know you can turn it off."

It's hard to enjoy the beauty of life when we are constantly plugged-in and connected. When was the last time you checked out of the matrix and realized that there's no rush and everything else can wait? Have you ever decided just to enjoy the moment, whatever it was? Hopefully, it was not too long ago. *Carpe diem,* my friend, or to borrow another quote from *Shawshank Redemption,* "Get busy living, or get busy dying."

I consider myself a foodie. There are few things on this earth like a good meal (no need to go into those). But if there is any time that you should take your time, it should be when you're eating a good meal. I travel a lot, and one of my personal rules for travel is that I avoid chain restaurants when visiting a new place. Why would I fly to a new city and eat a meal I could get back home? Makes no sense to me at all. In my eyes, it's borderline stupid.

In my travels, I have had some great meals; but I have also had some bad meals; so I've learned that when you find that place that gets it right, you have to linger and enjoy every bite. I am originally from Dallas, Texas, and one of my favorite steakhouses is there. So every time I'm at home, I make a point to go there. Usually, my meal is a two- to three-hour experience, and I enjoy everything along the way—wine, bread, appetizer, entrée, and dessert or a nice port, if not both. Many times, I am alone when I go, but when you throw great company and conversation into the equation, time ceases to exist.

What stops time for you? What activity or person allows you not to care about time and allows you to check out? There is no question that we all have to be productive in our jobs and in other areas, but we also can't be so much in a hurry that we don't allow ourselves to enjoy life, be it a meal, a car ride, an expensive wine, or just time with that person you love or enjoy the most.

Taking your time does not mean that you don't care about what's next. It simply highlights that what's going on in that moment takes precedence over everything else, and that's OK. Enjoy whatever or whomever it is, and when you are there, take your time!

Time to pour another drink.

HOW CAN YOU BETTER TAKE YOUR TIME AND ENJOY LIFE?

Chapter 9

WHAT THE HELL AM I DOING?

"What the hell am I doing here? I don't belong here."
Radiohead ("Creep")

When I was younger and there was an opportunity to get free drinks, I would not turn down anything. My mantra was always "You can't waste alcohol," and I made a point not to waste it, even it was to my detriment.

As I have gotten older, though, I have found that you can get a drink just about anywhere, especially if you are in a profession that is a big proponent of building and maintaining "client relationships," as in consulting, sales, and similar fields. On any given day, there is a cocktail reception somewhere, friends who want to buy a round, or just an open bottle that someone wants to share, so it becomes hard at times to say no because it's there, right? Maybe this is just my life and my friends, but you get the point.

There have been times when I found myself with a full glass of a spirit or wine that I didn't want, but since it was free, I felt compelled to drink it so I wouldn't be wasteful. A few years ago, I was at a reception with an open bar, and I made the most of it. But there was a point when I asked myself, *What the hell am I doing?* I didn't want anything else to drink and did not need anything else either. But there I was, continuing to drink because it was free.

I have a friend who always tells me, "Tim, there is no free lunch. Everything has a cost." The more I live, the more I realize that no truer words have been spoken. Beyond the irresponsible nature of continuing to drink at that reception when, clearly, I didn't want anymore, it means that when we put ourselves in situations like this, we are not healthy enough to ask ourselves, *What the hell am I doing?* and then stop. While it's easy to point to this night out, there were several other instances that had nothing to do with drinking when I asked myself that same question.

I love to travel. Because of the nature of my work, each year my travel has gradually increased; and I have acquired preferred status on my favorite airline, which has resulted in regular upgrades to first class. As is the case with most airlines, drinks are free when flying in the forward cabin. (Word of advice: Take the plastic cups. No telling when the glasses were last thoroughly cleaned. But that's another story for another day. Let's stay focused.)

A few years ago, I was flying back from a long weekend in Nassau, Bahamas, where I spent the better part of 72 hours gambling and drinking. As I was entering the airport, all I wanted to do was get home and rest, so I had every intention of sleeping on the flight home. As I checked in, I saw I had been upgraded. I knew then there was no way I could sleep. Instead, I thought how great of an opportunity this was to drink since they were going to be serving me drinks the whole flight.

As soon as I sat down, the flight attendant asked what I would like to drink. I immediately answered, "Bacardi and Ginger," forgetting about my desire to sleep or the hangover I was trying to shake off. For the next hour of the nearly two-hour flight, I drank. But halfway through the flight, I asked myself, *Why are you doing this? You said you wanted to sleep.*

Eventually, I told myself, *Enough is enough,* and asked for some water and went to sleep.

But I had to step back and figure out why I was drinking, knowing that I didn't even want those drinks. I realized that I was only drinking because free drinks were being served. They were there, so I had to drink. But "just because it's there" is never a good reason to do anything. As I have heard people say many times, "All money ain't good money."

I can think of many times when I have had to question my behavior as it relates to drinking, but the times when I have had to think about it had nothing to do with drinking. While I am happily married and have been for some years now, I can think back to my single days when I thought I was a ladies' man. Man, I had a run back in the day, but please don't let me drift from my point. I would like to think that any woman I shared my company with was marriage material, but I know that was far from the case.

There were plenty of times when I was in a conversation, out on a date, or even on the verge of an intimate moment when I asked myself, *Why am I here?* or *Why am I doing this?* These moments were not always a reflection on the other person. Rather, they were a reflection on decisions I made when I was not being honest with myself or I was not there for sincere reasons. As I have matured, I'm glad to say that I have limited the questionable decisions I've made, but there are still instances when I have to ask myself, *What the hell am I doing, and why?*

So while I'm questioning my drinking or the time I spent with a person I did not like that much, let me ask you, Why are you still in that job? Why are you buying that article of clothing you don't need, cheating on your diet, or doing any number of things that you have no business doing? Just because you can do something does not mean you need to be doing it. In the moment, it can seem to be innocent and no big deal, but the bigger question is, Why? Is this taking you away from goals you have set, potentially going to damage your character, or even put you in danger?

At the end of the day, it all comes down to discipline and focus. We see it every day, especially in this age of social media. It only takes one picture, one video, one wrong post, or an accusation for things to go wrong. So keep your focus. If you have a plan, don't let anything or anyone deter you from it. And be especially cautious if something is offered to you free because nothing in life is free. I have plenty of receipts to prove it.

WHEN WAS THE LAST TIME YOU QUESTIONED YOUR ACTIONS?

Chapter 10

IT'S OK TO BE ALONE

"It's hard to believe that there's nobody out there. It's hard to believe that I'm all alone. At least I have her love. The city, she loves me, lonely as I am. Together we cry." Red Hot Chili Peppers ("Under the Bridge")

I've heard people say, "If you are drinking alone, you have a problem." Really? What if no one is around? What if I want to be by myself? Or what if I've been talking all day and I'm sick of being around people? All of these sound like valid reasons to me to have a drink alone.

I can think of an endless number of great reasons, in my humble opinion, to drink alone, but I get it. I understand why people say the person who drinks alone may have a problem because most people who drink do so socially. Having said that, I've never had a problem being alone, so I surely have never had a problem drinking alone, especially if I have something expensive to drink that I don't want to share. Actually, I think it's perfectly OK to be alone and to reflect, rest, and reset. Sometimes it's good to shut out the noise, and that's more difficult to do when you're surrounded by people.

Too many times, people feel they can't be alone, especially when they are in a relationship. There is a certain amount of guilt that comes with expressing that you don't want to be around your partner or spouse. Sometimes it has to be done, but it needs to be done in a polite and gentle way.

I will go on record and say that marriage is the hardest thing I have ever done—ever—because marriage requires a person to be connected to someone else daily. And while I love being married, there is a certain amount of independence that can be lost in the union. I believe a healthy amount of independence allows us to be better partners, parents, and friends. I don't think my wife and I have ever had a formal conversation about it, but I think we both feel it's important to do things alone and independent of each other.

There are many instances when my wife and I plan trips, dinners, and other times when we simply do our own thing, and that's OK with us. Some people may look at this as a flaw in our marriage, but I have found it to be a strength and a solid foundation for our ten-year marriage.

Many times, people often comment and editorialize about how much I am out alone or ask where my wife is. But most of those people are single or divorced, so I take their commentary with a grain of salt. However, during these times, I am able to enjoy my own space, reenergize, and reflect. Ultimately, my time alone allows me to be a better person for my wife, my children, and everyone around me. The older I get, the more of an introvert I become, so personal time is a must on all levels.

I am a life-long runner, and I enjoy being on an open road on a beautiful day, running in the open air. Running is more than exercise or a hobby for me. Running helped pay my way through college as a scholarship athlete at Morehouse College, where I did long-distance, cross country, 5K, 10K, and occasionally steeplechase. Hell, it even helped me meet my wife.

By the end of my college career, I was an accomplished runner, winning multiple conference championships. But when my career was over, I just wanted to stop running because I had been doing it for so many years. After graduating from college, I did not run for about six months as I began graduate school at the University of Massachusetts, Amherst. But in that time, I fell into a dark place, and I could not figure out what was missing.

One day, while I was in this permanent funk, I told myself that I needed to get out and get a run. It was on that run that I found out how much running means to me, not because of the health benefits but because of the mental break it provides. For all those years, running was my therapy, and I didn't know it. During those runs was when I could think about schoolwork, reflect on life, work through conflicts, and have a moment to myself. Running was my alone time, and on that run, I found out how necessary it was for my overall personal health, not just my physical health.

As I move into my 40's, I still try to run two or three times a week. While it's not as easy as it used to be for many reasons, I find it to be more therapeutic than anything. Similarly, I have found that there are other things I like to do alone, not because I don't want to be around other people but because I enjoy my personal space. I've discovered that when I have alone time, I'm a better person for my family, friends, and coworkers.

Running may not be your thing. I know some people who enjoy knitting, reading, sailing, gaming, or numerous other activities. The key is to find what works for you, but I think everyone should have that thing that is theirs that allows them to reset, reflect, and rejuvenate. If your favorite activity allows you to unplug from all of the technology that at times can seem so suffocating, then all the better.

So, do I drink alone? Hell, yeah, I do and will do so as often as I like! And there is nothing wrong with it! Sometimes, I go to a bar, sit and people-watch, catch up on social media, or enjoy some good music alone. While I'm there, I may not say a word to anybody. Sometimes, I go to my back porch, my favorite place, and sit in a rocking chair. Or I might sit in a hotel room with a bottle of wine, watching *SportsCenter* and unwinding after a long day in my travels as opposed to being out. In any of these instances, I feel at peace, and it allows me to reset.

In my opinion, it's OK to be alone. It's in those moments when I have discovered the most about myself, and I have time to think about the world around me in an uninterrupted way, which allows me to be the best me. Do you have a space to be alone? Do you like to be alone? When was the last time you were truly alone? It may not be your thing, but if it isn't, don't knock it for those of us who crave our personal space and alone time.

WHEN DID YOU LAST ENJOY SOME GOOD "ME TIME"?

Chapter 11

CASH IS KING

"Cash rules everything around me. C.R.E.A.M., get the money, dollar, dollar bill, y'all." Wu Tang Clan ("C.R.E.A.M.")

"Keep it open, or close it out?" I've been asked that on numerous occasions, and most times my response is "Yes, keep it open," or better yet, "Run it." Running a tab is convenient for many reasons. You don't have to worry about digging in your pocket for cash every time you want to buy a drink, but it also limits the number of people behind the bar you have to interact with. Instead, you can establish a rapport with a single bartender, which potentially can pay dividends down the road in the form of a better pour, a free drink, or just some good solid advice. I have learned a lot of good things from bartenders, most notably the importance of tipping.

However, opening a tab also, in many instances, takes away your ability to track your spending. I think we all can agree that after a couple of rounds, judgment and fiscal responsibility can go out the door very quickly. What starts out as just having a couple of drinks with friends can quickly become hundreds of dollars of drinks before you know it. I can't tell you how many times I have found receipts in my pockets or looked online at my account from the previous night and asked, "What the hell did I buy?"

This has happened to me many times and is one of the reasons I have more credit card debt than I care to have at this stage of my life. Where cash does not provide the conveniences of credit, it does allow the ability to better track spending and ensure that, ultimately, I get what I pay for. Some bartenders try to get over on people who run tabs by charging them extra, thinking the patrons will not catch it, which has happened to me. Maybe these were honest mistakes, but it further supports the argument that things like that don't happen when you use cash. With cash, once you pay $15.00 for that drink, you are done, as opposed to the accruing credit card interest, which can cost you more than the actual drink or the final bill in the long run.

In a bar, prices are pretty much set, but in most other places, there is a distinct difference between the cash and credit prices. You can see this at gas stations and some liquor stores, in addition to other places where they differentiate the price between cash and credit as market conditions fluctuate. I am not telling you anything you don't already know, but merchants are charged for each transaction they process. While larger chain merchants can absorb this cost, smaller business owners would rather not, so some of them have minimum charges to use a credit card so that they won't have to absorb that cost. (Little secret: They aren't supposed to do this.)

When cash is involved, people rarely pay the sticker price, especially with big-ticket items. If you walk into a car dealership tomorrow and are not limited by what you can pay and do not need financing, you will pay nothing close to the listed price. This also holds true for houses, jewelry, and many of the things most people have to finance.

I was talking to one of my friends about this topic, and he said, "Credit is for broke people." At the time, I thought he was being rather harsh and elitist, but when I reflected on it, I realized he had a valid and fair point. Not to diminish the need for credit in some instances, but the reality is that there are some people who choose not to use credit, but they have the money to do so.

Another colleague of mine talked about how his great-uncle did not believe in buying insurance, because if something went wrong, he had the money to fix it. (This was in a different time before there were so many insurance regulations.) In both instances, the reality is that if you have the capital or cash, you are in a place of power and are not at the mercy of any person or financial institution and their terms.

The reality is that most of us do need access to credit and financing at some point in time, but most of the time, it's used for wants, not needs. How many people can buy a house or a car outright or afford not to have insurance? So while it would be good to do so, it's just not realistic. But there are still plenty of places where having cash in your hand can make a difference.

Many of us live in a world where a $20, $50, or $100 handshake or tip can make a big difference. One of the first lessons I learned when I was entering the workforce was that people in charge rarely know what's going on. So if you want to make something happen, you are better off talking to an administrative assistant, custodial worker, or security guard than the manager or the CEO. This is especially true in the service and hospitality industry. If you want a good seat at a restaurant, you could call ahead to be told they are booked for the night, or you could show up with some cash and get the best seat in the place.

One night, I was at a black-tie affair, and there was wine for the table. But as the program was coming to an end, the waiter came over and asked if there was anything else we needed. One of the men sitting at the table put $50 in the server's hand and said, "We want to continue to enjoy the night." Within minutes, six bottles of wine arrived at the table, and the server said, "Enjoy."

Now if we had asked someone in management, there would have been some drawn-out conversation. But since we talked to the person who actually knew what was going on and how things flowed, we were well taken care of. And for transactions like that, a credit card won't do.

There is also a lot of leverage to be gained through the use of cash, but I would be remiss if I didn't discuss the reality of when cash is the only option for any number of reasons. Some places don't take credit, and there are other times when you don't want to use credit. Some view cash as being beneficial, because in some instances, once you complete your transaction, it's done. For some people, this is ideal because not all transactions need to have a history. In a world driven by technology, where everything has a history and is tracked and recorded, it's good to know that some things can't be tracked. And in that world, cash will always be king to some people and markets.

So as they ask in the Capital One commercials, "What's in your wallet?" While you may have a wallet or a purse full of credit cards with excessive limits ready to keep that tab open, I would suggest that you also keep some cash on hand as well in case you want to track your spending, need to negotiate, don't want your transaction to have a trail, or just want to have some tip money. I know several people who insist on keeping between $50 to $100 on them at all times just in case. It is always good to have options. You never know when a credit card machine may be down or how far a handshake with some cash in it can go!

DO YOU REGULARLY CARRY CASH? IF NOT, WHY?

Chapter 12

A CLOSED MOUTH DOESN'T GET FED

"You need to git up, git out, and git somethin'. How will you make it if you never even try? You need to git up, git out, and git somethin'. 'Cuz you and I got to do for you and I." Outkast ("Git Up, Git Out")

If you don't ask, you'll never know the answer. It's just that simple. Hotels, rental car companies, bars and restaurants, and several other industries operate with room for a lot of capacity to be able to keep up with demand. But many times, they have a lot of unused inventory that they are looking to unload if possible.

When I check into a hotel or rent a car, one of the first things I ask the attendant is if there is an upgrade available. Sometimes, they come back with a price for the upgrade, but many times they accommodate me for free. What did I lose in asking for the upgrade? Nothing. But many times, I was upgraded to a nicer car or room just by simply asking a question.

Outside of peak times, inventory often goes unused, so from the company's perspective, it's not a loss. Instead, it's an opportunity to improve your experience, increasing the chance that you will come back. So what do they have to lose from a customer service standpoint?

Many times, I have been at a bar and asked, "Do you have any specials?" Often, there are specials, depending on the time of day and if you ask. But if you say nothing, they won't say anything either because what you don't know can't hurt you. In that same vein, I have also found that talking to bartenders is a good way to get faster service, a better pour, and sometimes even comped drinks.

On my 41st birthday, I was out with some friends. We started up a casual conversation with Douglas, our bartender, and it came up that it was my birthday. Douglas asked what I was drinking. That night, I happened to be drinking Don Julio 1942 tequila, which can run $40.00 or more for a pour. But that night, Douglas comped one of my drinks, all from just engaging him in the conversation.

Now let me be clear. I am not saying you should go around hoping or expecting to get things for free, because there is no free lunch! I'm simply saying that amazing opportunities will often open up when you say something. I think back over my life and see that some of the best moments and opportunities that have happened came from me asking or making an inquiry.

One of my closest friends is responsible for special events at a resort, and for years he hosted a celebrity event there. To him it was work, so he dreaded it, but for me it was an opportunity to see how the stars and the top 1% play. Often, he would tell me about the event, so finally I asked if he could get me in. He said it would be no problem. Not only was I able to go to the event, but I was also able to get behind-the-scenes access to the resort, along with all of the weekend's events.

Ultimately, I attended this event every year for over ten years until they stopped hosting it. But during that time, I was able to meet some of the biggest stars in the world and made several memories that I will never forget. I could take this time to name drop, but I'll just say that I met several cool people.

While the act of simply asking can potentially get you significant perks and benefits, I think it is far more important to open your mouth to ask for help in a time of need. Many times, it's the people who need help the most who say the least. Almost every day, we hear of instances of people being abused or bullied, going through addiction, or struggling with any number of situations where they need help. But because they don't say anything, many times, their situations get worse and, in some instances, have fatal endings.

I used to be over a university resource center that helped students get academic assistance. At the end of the semester, we had to evaluate the program and see who was using our academic support services. What we found in our evaluations was that students who needed the help the least used the services the most, and students who needed it the most used it the least.

During my final year at the resource center, I found out that the student who used the services the most had a 3.9 GPA and was on his way to medical school, while many of the students on academic probation that semester had never used our services at all. This was especially problematic because the support services were free. I admit that there are many factors that can influence whether someone asks for help, but it does not change the fact that saying nothing is never good and is often detrimental.

There are many times when you can say something to someone and get a negative response or no response at all. None of us like the idea of rejection or being told no, especially me. I hate it. But on the other hand, if you never ask, you will never know what can happen. If you are happy with that place or situation, then say nothing. But if you want something a little bit better, or if you want a different perspective, say something and don't worry about what could happen. Hope for the best.

I am an eternal optimist. I always see the glass as half full, so why not ask? What's the worst that could happen? My life is much better for opening my mouth for upgrades and help. When I think back on some of my best times, upgrades and a few drinks are just a couple of the many great things and experiences I have received by just asking. Beyond those things, I have also received great professional opportunities and good advice as well.

WHEN DID YOU LAST ASK FOR HELP OR FOR A FAVOR FROM SOMEONE?

Chapter 13

TIME VS. MONEY

"All for the love of money. Don't let, don't let, don't let money rule you." The O'Jays ("For the Love of Money")

As I have grown older, I have found that time is limited and, yes, it eventually will run out on all of us. You can have all the money in the world, but time is something that you cannot buy. While time and money have unbelievable value, I have learned to invest more in how I use time than in worrying about money.

So what does this have to do with drinking? Well, because of the nature of my work, which includes lots of networking opportunities and social outings, I end up being invited to places where drinks are plentiful. There was a time in my life when I would not have dared to miss an event that had an open bar. If you mentioned free drinks, I was there. But now, the attraction of free drinks and nice venues is no longer as tempting if I have better things to do with my time, like spending time with friends or family; resting; or just doing nothing, which happens so rarely. It seems like there is always something that needs to be done.

In any given week, I work between 40-60 hours. I leave the office, deal with Atlanta traffic after carpool, come home to my children and my wife, and manage a small business. But somewhere among all those things, I try to find a little "me time," which tends to happen late at night or early in the morning. Since I don't like getting up in the morning, that means there are a lot of late nights for me. With such a packed schedule, social events and cocktail hours don't have the same luster they used to have. And most of the time, it's an extension of work, so I have come to the conclusion that during those times I could be doing other things.

The dilemma of time vs. money also plays out in public forums as well with celebrities and other high-profile people. In an age where everyone is trying to get rich, it has become normal for someone to come up with a frivolous lawsuit to try and get a quick buck. While some people fight such lawsuits, there are others who settle out of court because once they figure in the time and energy it takes to go back and forth, the court costs, and the possibility of dragging the story out, many just pay the problem to go away. Why? Because in most cases, the amount of money being asked for in the lawsuit is nominal, and these people just want to get on with their lives.

I once heard a story of a celebrity who had a separate account for such cases in order to avoid wasting time in court. While we cannot all just shell out thousands, and sometimes millions, of dollars, we can learn to protect our time. In the end, your time is one of the few things that is really yours.

Anyone who has been in a relationship long enough has maybe had an argument or two with a partner or close friends. One of the most animated arguments—or should I say, passionate discussions—I have had with my wife was over going to brunch with some of her friends.

I was coming off a long period of travel during one of my busiest times of the year and had just finished a week with a few major deadlines for work, so I was looking forward to a Saturday to just chill around the house and not have to be "on." But she was insistent that we go because the brunch would only last two hours. My counterargument was that those were my two hours. Besides, when you factor in travel time and talkative people, would it really be two hours? No! Not to be deterred, she even tried to coax me to go by telling me they would have plenty to drink there. And? My rebuttal to that was I have plenty to drink here at home.

After days of going back and forth about this brunch, I finally gave in. You learn to pick and choose your battles in marriage. I went, but just as I had said, the brunch lasted far longer than two hours. The whole time I was there, I couldn't help but think of all the other things I would have rather done with my time than sit around eating brunch.

Speaking of eating, one of my favorite places to eat in Atlanta does not take reservations and doesn't even have a host stand. For years, this place has been one of the most successful restaurants in the city. Anyone who has a party of more than two people has to wait in line, and I have seen people wait for as long as 45 minutes to an hour with no problem.

The first time I went to this restaurant, I wondered why anyone would wait so long to order their food without sitting down. But I discovered that the food was great, and later someone explained to me that the same 30-45 minutes that I waited in line is the same 45 minutes, in many instances, that I would spend sitting down waiting for a waiter to take my order and bring out the food. I have found out that the service model is predicated on getting people in and out. Now it doesn't hurt that the food is great, but it also helps that I know that outside of peak business hours, I can get a great meal in less than 30 minutes—less if I'm alone.

Whenever I'm there, I see people from all walks of life—a police officer who only has a few minutes, a housewife who is catching up with a friend, or a group of co-workers who have a set time for lunch. Of course, the food is what brings them in, but it's knowing that they can get in and out in a timely manner that also keeps people coming back. The extensive selection of tequilas doesn't hurt either, in my opinion!

So protect what little time you have at all cost. There will always be events that come up that you cannot get out of, but be firm on not wasting your time on other things that you are genuinely not interested in. I have heard some say that time is a valuable commodity, but I would argue that time is priceless.

WHAT DO YOU VALUE THE MOST?

Chapter 14

VICES

"Maybe you're just like my mother. She's never satisfied."
Prince ("When Doves Cry")

For the past 20 years, I have traveled to Nassau, Bahamas, a couple of times a year if possible. This has become my happy place. During the many times I've traveled there, I've participated in Junkanoo, the most popular folk art expression in the Bahamas, and attended many events at Atlantis, such as the grand opening of The Cove. I was also a fixture at The Annual Michael Jordan Celebrity Golf Tournament. Most importantly, I got married to my beautiful wife in Nassau in 2007.

I have so many great memories of Nassau, all of which can't be shared, but I also learned some great lessons such as not to mix vices. For me, that means not to mix liquor and gambling in the same day. This has rarely, if ever, worked out for me in my 20 years going to Nassau. I have had to learn that the hard way. Thus, I have learned to pick one and stick with it.

The Collins Dictionary defines a *vice* as "a habit that is regarded as a weakness in someone's character, but not usually a serious fault." While we have established that I may have at least one vice, there are a few more that I have to work hard to control, including gambling.

All my life, I've competed in basketball, football, soccer, tennis, along with track and field and cross country in college, so losing has never been an option for me. It's always my goal to win everything I do. But I can't tell you how much money I have won or lost in Nassau at Atlantis Casino. Maybe I helped finance the building of The Cove. What I can tell you is that when I drink *and* gamble, it doesn't end well because my competitive nature gets the better of me, and at times I have lost all control.

While most of the times I have gambled I have had supervision in the form of my wife or friends, I remember at least one late night I was alone and decided to try my luck before I took it in for the night.

After about 30 minutes (more like 15), I was down a few hundred dollars at the craps table. (I think.) I had been drinking all day. Somehow, I just knew I was about to get hot and was just one roll away from getting it all back. But after four trips to the ATM, I had reached my daily limit and couldn't get any more money.

Then I realized that maybe I had done too much, but I was in denial, so I called my wife back in the States and asked her if something was wrong with my card. She logged onto our account and, well, let's just say that that conversation didn't go well at all! I think her exact words were, "Take your drunk ass to your room! How the hell do you lose that much money in 30 minutes?" At that point, I had no choice but to head back to my room. But I did get one more drink for the road. They owed me that at least, right?

In over 20 years in my professional career in higher education, I've had the opportunity to work with hundreds of great students that ranged from former felons to Rhodes scholars, all who went on to do great things. While I don't remember them all, there are a few who stand out. One of them is James. I worked with him during my time at Atlanta Metropolitan State College, which used to be a junior college. James was a bright young man who could have gone to any number of four-year colleges, but because of his situation, he felt that a two-year college was a good starting point for him.

The first time I met him, I knew he was different. He often came by my office and talked about school, life, and his career goals. He loved cars, and they were beyond a passion for him. But I don't think he realized just how much of a passion they were. At the time, his pet project was rebuilding an old muscle car. One day, he stopped by my office, frustrated about his financial situation. He said it seemed that he never had enough money. He told me that he didn't go to clubs, buy expensive clothes, or waste money like many other students did.

Finally, I stopped him and asked how much he had spent on rebuilding his car that month. He gave me a puzzled look. I asked him again. He thought about it and said, "I think, about $1,500." I told him that the money he spent on that car counts, too, even if he wasn't throwing it away on other things. He admitted that he had never thought about it that way because to him spending money on his car wasn't wasteful. It was more of an investment. He might have been right about that, but because he was spending so much money on the car and didn't have enough money for other things, that car had become his vice.

In the same way, many people have vices and may not even realize it. There's nothing necessarily wrong with having vices, but here are my suggestions for dealing with them. First, find out what your personal vices are. You can't control them if you don't know what they are. Second, if you find that you have more than a handful of vices, limit them to three. Third, don't mix vices. It usually never ends well.

While in Nassau, I often tried to mix my vices. I've won a lot of money gambling when I was focused and sober. I've also had some great days drinking and having fun with my friends. But I've had very few days when I could do both successfully at the same damn time.

Put simply, vices are our passions—at least the healthy ones are. But there is a slippery slope between a passion and an addiction. It all comes down to control. I think we all should have something we enjoy and are passionate about.

I admired James and his passion for cars, so when I pointed out how much money he was spending, it wasn't a criticism. It was an observation. If he didn't recognize how much he was spending on rebuilding the car and that his spending was bleeding over into other parts of his budget, that's when it became problematic, just like my doomed evening gambling.

Do you know your vices? Can you control them? If not, I encourage you to think about what is holding you back and stopping you from reaching your personal goals of saving money, losing weight, or making major changes in your life. Be honest with yourself as you think about your vices and how you can limit them and better control them.

My vices are travel, drinking, and gambling, which is why Nassau is not only my happy place, but sometimes it's a major problem, given that it's just a little over a two-hour flight from Atlanta. So in my 20 years of going there, I've learned recently to pick two of my vices because when all three are in motion, it doesn't work out for me or my bank account!

OK, it's last call. One more drink, and then we have to take it in.

WHAT ARE YOUR VICES?

Chapter 15

LAST CALL

"Good things come to those that wait up, but don't wait to jump in too long. Don't sleep. You gotta stay up." Miguel ("Sky Walker")

Throughout this book, I have shared a few random and appropriate adventures I have experienced through drinking and my travels with the hope of providing some laughter but also insights about how these principles can be applied to other aspects of our lives beyond cocktails. I talk to one of my closest friends a couple of times a week via text, and we try to get together a couple of times a month or whenever time allows. When I ask how he is doing, often his reply is, "Living and learning, brother." I laugh and keep the conversation moving, but one day I asked what he meant by that. He said that life is always trial and error, trying to figure things out, which makes complete sense when you think about it.

In many of this book's chapters, there is a lesson to be learned through trial and error. There is no substitute for experience. Whether it involves knowing your enemy, figuring out who your friends are, or when it's the right time to walk away, these are all things we have to figure out on our own. Someone close to me once told me, "Lessons are repeated until they are learned." I have had plenty of lessons, but I have had to figure a lot of them out on my own. While I have presented just a few lessons, I have learned that there are plenty I am still trying to figure out.

Another part of living and learning is the idea of just being awake and in the moment. Many times, the answer we are seeking is right there in front of our faces, but we are too busy or not attuned to what is going on, not paying attention, in denial, or distracted by all the crap life can throw at us. I will not go into any faith talk, but many times, there are larger powers at work. And if we remain still and go with our gut, have faith, trust in the Spirit, and follow our instincts or whatever you want to call it, the guidance we are looking for often presents itself if we are attentive to hear or receive it.

In 2000, I graduated with a master's degree and was dead-set on not taking a job unless I could make a certain salary or have a certain amount of prestige. Months went by, and I didn't get the offers I was looking for. During all that time that I was waiting on the right (perfect) job conditions, I blew through all my savings and had to work temp jobs for hourly wages that were less than what I made in high school eight years earlier when I was an assistant manager at a yogurt shop. So the lesson is, beware when you are waiting on the "perfect" anything.

This was one of the most humbling times in my life and one that I will never forget. I didn't reach out to anyone because I wanted to do it all on my own. Finally, one of my friends heard that I was looking for a job and talked with someone else. That person called me and asked me to bring in a resume on my lunch break. Worried about the time it would take, I went back and forth about if I would go. Ultimately, I decided to take the resume and was offered a position doing something that I enjoyed in my professional field.

I often tell people that I have not worked a day in the past 15 years. This opportunity was always in front of me, but I was not awake because I was too focused on numbers and titles to open my eyes to the resources that I had right before me, which speaks to "a closed mouth doesn't get fed."

At the end of the day, nothing is certain, nothing is guaranteed. We are all just trying to figure out this thing called life. What I have shared in my book are hard lessons that I have learned through numerous cocktails and a "few" bad decisions, but I have learned a lot from it all and am a better person because of some of these experiences. If I had it to do all over again, I would not change a thing. Well, maybe I would have not drunk so much gin that night at that house party. But you know what? Everything happens as it should.

There is no telling how much money I could have saved or how my life would have been different without these experiences or that first sip of that Fuzzy Navel, but I know I am right where I need to be. I have no doubt that I have invested more in spirits than I care to admit; but at this point in my life, I look back at all I have learned from these lessons and remain confident that they will pay dividends for years to come.

Every year, people ask me if I have any New Year's resolutions. My answer is simply that I want to be better next year than I was last year and just to continue living and learning from it all!

Thanks for hanging out for a few drinks. Time to take it in. 'Night!

WHAT IS THE BIGGEST LESSON YOU HAVE LEARNED IN THE LAST YEAR?

www.ingramcontent.com/pod-product-compliance
Lightning Source LLC
Chambersburg PA
CBHW060548310726
48982CB00008B/1055/J

* 9 7 8 0 9 9 7 4 3 1 8 6 5 *